HERO GIRLS

About the Author

Bernard Ashley lives in Charlton, south-east London, only a street or so from where he was born. Bernard wrote throughout his career as a teacher and headteacher and is now writing full time.

He has written more than twenty full-length novels for young people - and over fifty books in all including picture book texts. He has written television serials including 'Running Scared', 'Dodgem', and the one-off 'Justin and the Demon Drop Kick'.

Bernard is particularly known for the vivid way he reflects our multi-cultural cities, and many of his books have been short-listed for prizes.

He is a popular visitor to schools and libraries, performing lively sessions for children of all ages.

You c̶a̶n̶ ̶v̶i̶s̶i̶t̶ ̶B̶e̶r̶n̶a̶r̶d̶ ̶a̶t̶ ̶h̶i̶s̶ ̶w̶ebsite at

Also by Bernard Ashley

Your Guess is as Good as Mine
Justin and the Demon Drop Kick

HERO GIRLS

BERNARD ASHLEY

Published by Ashley Chappel Productions
128 Heathwood Gardens, London SE7 8ER, UK

This edition first published 2012
1 3 5 7 9 10 8 6 4 2

A CIP catalogue record for this book is available from the
British Library

ISBN 978 0 9570357 2 0

Production by **author**ization!
E: martin-west@btconnect.com

Printed in Poland

CONTENTS

'Monday Morning' was first published in *I'm Trying to Tell You* (Kestrel Books) in 1981

'A Picture of Home' was first published in *Stacks of Stories* (a Library Assocation Anthology) in 1997, with thanks to Yasim Elmi

'Stronger than Sprite' has been especially written for *Hero Girls* in 2012

'Sally Cinderella' was first published in 1989 (Orchard)

'Boat Girl' was first published in 1990 (Julia MacRae Books), with thanks to Thinh and Ly Ung

MONDAY MORNING

'Nerissa Jones, what *are* you thinking about? You're certainly not thinking about writing a story for me.'

Miss Banks sat frowning away down that room like she'd left her contacts out. Sour as a green apple, she was.

'Raymond Smith's done a page already. What have you done?'

There weren't no point in tellin' no lies. My bit of paper was as blank as that wall, and I didn't have no more idea of some 'Exciting Adventure' than that desk lid.

'I'm thinking 'bout my sister, Miss,' I said.

'Well, there's a time and a place for everything,' she comes back. 'Now get your mind on your work, girl.'

So I tried—but it's really hard, concentrating on story writing when your mind's all buzzing with other things. It's like a glass door, inside your brain, I reckon. You can shut it hard as you like, but them other thoughts still keep showing through.

I could still see all their faces, and all the fussing and the clapping, and the smart, best turn-outs. I could see my sister in her bride-frock, looking like the queen of all the world. And my daddy's smiling mouth—and his crying eyes.

And looking down, like I did a million times Saturday, I could still see my pink silk shoes, shining when I danced.

And now I was sitting at my desk, looking this time at those legs I'd had before, and the little white socks and the old brown bumpers.

You don't stay special for long, do you? It don't seem five minutes before you're back to your old self again, doing sums and having to think up Exciting Adventures.

There's been talking for weeks about how my sister has her hair. 'No fussing,' my mammy says, 'just neat with a pretty ribbon there.'

'You are joking, ain't you?' my sister says. And she threatens something *drastic* if she hears any more of that talk.

She has what she wants in the end: beautiful blown-out curls, looking like a flower in the moonlight.

When I see her coming down the stairs, I can't tell you how I feel. I want to smile till my face splits, and cry a bucket of tears, and there's this new feeling of no floor beneath my feet. And I can't breathe, too. I just stand there with my mouth open, making some funny noise or other.

And I think, 'Is this what happens, then? That girl in the next-door bed to mine—she leaves it in a heap every morning and grumbles in her sleep, and she never can find her shoes—does she come out like this, one day? Like a beautiful butterfly out of a tangly bush?'

And then riding in that big car to the church, that's something special, with those pink ribbons fluttering like they're waving hello to people. You keep your eyes on your shoes, but you're really thinking, 'It's me in here; and why can't my mates all be out in the street this Saturday morning?'

My mammy's with me; not crying. She's been keeping too busy to think about what's really happening, I reckon.

But I take a sideways look, and I wonder if she might be having a think back to *her* wedding day. Different from this, going by the picture. Outside a little church in Kingston back home, where the sunny white wall made the whole world look brilliant and bright.

I s'pose she must've been thinking along the same lines, because she suddenly says, 'Well, at least that old sun's putting on a show.' And I reckon it was. It made Clapham brighten up and smile. And my mammy sits back in her seat instead of perching nervous on the front; and she closes her eyes and mumbles something quiet.

So it's all going well according to the plans. I'm the happiest person in the world except my sister; Auntie Lizzie's gone in the first car; our car's running to time; and there's just my daddy and the beautiful bride waiting for the first driver to double back and get them. Everything's perfect.

Except we turn round the corner up to the church and there isn't a living soul there.

'There ain't no wedding here today,' the driver says, sliding back his glass. 'This place is all shut up, missus.'

'That can't be the case,' my mammy says. 'Perhaps they've all gone in and shut the doors.'

'Hey, you sure this is the right day?' the driver asks. 'Give me a look of your invitation.'

'I ain't got no invitation!' my mammy snaps. 'I'm the mother of the bride. I don't get issued with no invitation. And what d'you think I am, stupid? Not knowing the right day of my own daughter's wedding? And where's that first car gone?'

The driver shrugs his shoulders. 'Search me. But there ain't no wedding here, that's for sure. I've never seen a place look so closed up and empty.'

I was getting real edgy with this driver now. He had the look on him that, all right, we were sitting in his car, and he did have to care a bit about our problem, but he wasn't going to move no mountains for us.

'What's the name of this church you've brought us to?' I ask him. He gives me this long stare. It's a good job for him my daddy ain't in this car, I'm thinking. He wouldn't be sitting there all don't-care if he was.

'Saint Thomas's,' he says, resting his hands on the steering-wheel. 'That's the address your fellow gave us.'

I come to, then. 'Well, I can tell you this ain't Saint Thomas's,' I tell him. 'I go to Sunday School at Saint Thomas's, and there's no way this is that place.'

The driver said nothing, but he started pointing at the notice board, all slow and cocky.

THE CHURCH OF SAINT THOMAS, CLAPHAM COMMON, it said.

'Well, what are you doing, then?' I asked him, giving my mammy and me both a surprise. 'Saint Thomas, Clapham *Junction* is what we want.'

He didn't say no more. Just muttered a bit. But didn't he drive fast, now he knew it was his mistake! One pink ribbon came off, and the other was flapping and flying like a streamer. People had to jump out of the way just to save their skins. My mammy closed her eyes and knocked her hat on the tilt.

You should have heard the cheers when we got ourselves there.

The bride was waiting already and my daddy was walking in all directions at once. But did their faces start to smile!

Uncle Ben stopped it being a nasty turn-out with the car people.

'You gone the long way round buying peppers?' he says to my mammy. 'You don't need to make such a big fuss of me.'

And then it all went forward like the stories tell. I carried the bride's train and never tripped, and stepped up and back when the moments came. And everyone was happy. We sang, our families, like old Saint Thomas Clapham Junction ain't never heard before. And back at home we sang and danced so hard, I never noticed I slept on my own in that bedroom till the next afternoon around two.

Now I can't get it out of my head, no matter what tricks I try. School Monday

morning is all mixed up. I get the words
of 'Once upon a time' down on that
paper, but nothing else; and then Miss
Banks is there, going on again.

'This just isn't good enough,' she says.
'Really, Nerissa Jones – haven't you got
any ideas for an exciting story?'

A PICTURE OF HOME

Ugaso Samatar looked round the big classroom. It had more than thirty children in it; but there were no other Somali children, no-one else who spoke her language.

'*Aabe!*' It was real scary, being in Britain. Not scary like running away from the stench of burning villages or the sound of shooting. And not scary like trying to get behind a stunted thorn-bush, hiding from the rival clansmen with her mother and little brother. But scary in other ways.

There was the noise of London – the lorries which rattled like troop carriers, and the buses which suddenly hissed their brakes like rockets skimming overhead. And those low aeroplanes, coming into the City Airport – which still had Ugaso's mother ducking her head as if they might be carrying bombs.

And there was another sort of scary which was just as bad, in its own way. The scare of being on their own, the three of them, the flats where they lived, as high as kites fly. The three of them without Ugaso's father, Yasin, who'd got them out of Hargeisa and on to the trail across the mountains before he went off to fight against the other clan. On their own without a word of English.

But Ugaso's father had been a teacher, and he spoke good English; and if only he were here, it would help them in this foreign land.

Ugaso came to school every day and tried like mad to understand what people were saying. But at night she cried for her father and stained her face with tears.

She dreamed one special dream – of one day going to the airport with her mother and brother, and seeing him coming through that door from where the aeroplanes land. Come to make them all together again. After that, everything would be a million times better.

Ugaso's teacher, who was a kind man, clapped his hands. Ugaso sat up straight, on the instant. He clapped his hands again, and one by one the others stopped what they were doing and started to listen to him.

'Xx'xx xxxxx xx xxx xxxxxxx,' he said. It meant nothing to Ugaso. He looked especially at her and opened and closed his hands like the opening and closing of a book. 'Xxxxx,' he said.

Ugaso thought she understood. It was something about books. But it wasn't going to happen in here, because all the others were scraping back chairs, getting books out of their trays and lining up with them at the classroom door. The class was going somewhere else.

Ugaso looked in her own tray for a book and took out the only one she had, a Maths book.

'Xxx xxxx!' Patti on her table was shaking her head, as if Ugaso were a bit stupid. She took the book off her and put it back in the tray. 'Xxxx xx.' She did a 'come on' with a finger, and a jerk with her head. 'Xxxx xx.'

That had to mean, 'Come with me', or something like it.

Ugaso went, and put herself on the end

of the line of children at the door, all of them holding onto books, except her.

This school had three floors, with lots of little landings and rooms in between. Not a bit like Ugaso's old school, in Hargeisa. Her Islamic school back home had been long and low and painted in a smooth white wash – until the looters had come and the flames had blackened it.

This London school had lots of small bricks in patterns, and from the yard outside it seemed to go up high enough to scrape the bellies of the aeroplanes as they went over. So much of London went *up* instead of *along*.

Ugaso's class led on down the stairs, round and round – everyone talking, some jumping, till suddenly the teacher stopped the lot of them.

'Xxx xxxxx! Xx xx xxx'x xx xxxxx xx'xx xx xxxx xxx xxx'x xxxxxx xxx books.'

Ugaso smiled. That last word she recognised. *Books.*

'Books,' she said to Patti. Now she knew where they were. It was a *maktabad*, a library. They went inside. It wasn't a lot different to the library in her old school in Hargeisa, except it was bigger. And this one didn't just have books. All down one side of the room there was a line of tables with computers on them.

The teacher sat at a teachers' table and marked off the books the others were giving back. The children went off to choose new ones, in between laughing and pulling faces through the shelves. Till he clapped his hands again, loud as a gunshot, and shouted at them, like a warrior.

'Xxx, xxx, xxx xxx!' He pointed at three

children. 'Xxxx XXXXX, xx xxx xxxx!' The three went and stood by the door, hanging their heads – but smiling at the floor.

Ugaso wasn't smiling, though. No way! She had shivered, and all at once she was crying. It had been just like that day her father had told her about; when the teachers had been lined up in the school yard like bad children, and 'You, you and you!' the government soldiers had shouted. And Ugaso always thanked Allah that her father hadn't been one of them. Because the chosen three had been marched off round a corner, and a gun had fired, three times.

'X'x xxxxx, Ugaso.' The teacher had come over and was offering a tissue from the box on the table. He was bending to her, putting his hands together as if in prayer, asking her to forgive him. 'Come with me. Come on.'

She went with him. Even through her tears she understood those words. But she knew she couldn't *start* to make him understand what had made her cry. Perhaps one day she would, when her English was better, if she could ever bear to tell him. If she could bear to think about how much danger her father was still in, fighting those other clansmen – shooting a gun, and having guns shooting against him.

The teacher took her to a computer and loaded a disc. 'Patti, come xxx xxxx.'

Patti came over. She was smiling, one of those double sorts of smiles, both at being picked to help; and a little bit of showing-off for knowing how to work this thing.

Ugaso looked at Patti, who was staring at the screen without blinking; not saying anything with her mouth, but her face saying she was going to surprise Ugaso with something. It had the cool look of Ugaso's father doing one of his magic tricks.

And she suddenly turned to Ugaso as if she had invented rice and maize. Ugaso looked at the computer screen.

In front of her was a page of unreadable writing; but what grabbed her eye was a picture. A picture she knew.

A picture from Somalia! There was no mistaking it – a scene of acacia trees by a stream, and a woman with a pot on her head coming to get water, and in the background, camels. Overhead, the sky was clear and blue, with no shell-burst clouds or rocket trails. Ugaso could almost hear the peaceful bleating of sheep.

He mouth opened, and a Somali sound clicked in her throat. Her eyes closed in a 'thank-you' and she gave a smile of great pleasure.

This picture was of the northern lands. This was what it was like, outside the town, where the animals were grazed.

Ugaso sat, and she stared. Patti reached for the mouse to change the screen, but Ugaso stopped her with a word she found she knew.

'No.'

The picture stayed; and although it didn't move, when Ugaso half-closed her eyes, it seemed to come to life and she could almost see her father walking down through those acacia trees swinging a bucket to get water of his own – and laughing the way he did when things were the way they ought to be.

'Xx xx xxxx?' The teacher had come to look at the picture, too. He was asking her a question, Ugaso could tell that. He squinted as the text and ran his finger along the line of acacia trees on the screen.

'Acacia xxxxx,' he said.

'Acacia,' said Ugaso; but more like 'a-cass-ia'.

'Trees,' he said.

'Trees.' Now she knew that word, too.

And her smile told him she had what she wanted. A picture of home.

That night, in the high flat, Ugaso had a new dream. It wasn't of her father at the airport, but of her father in the computer picture, still coming down through the acacia trees. But before he ever got close enough for her to hear his laugh or to touch his hand, he disappeared.

Ugaso woke, and turned her pillow to the dry side; and, without waking her mother, she went to the bedroom window.

It was always the same in London;

day or night it was bright. Looking out she could see the river Thames and the tall buildings alongside it. The city. Their new home, because there was no going back to Somalia until all the clan fighting had stopped. And yet not their true home.

It was a week before Library Time again; a week in which Ugaso learned lots of new words in *English*. Now she could say 'me' and 'you' and 'ta'. And, in one of the little rooms on a turn of the staircase, she had lessons in English from Mrs Hussein, who came in just for her.

But while the muscles which make words worked all right, the muscles which make smiles were never used.

Until Library Time. When they went to change books again – Ugaso had had a picture book without words – she went direct to a computer and sat down.

'Xx, I know xxxx you like.' Mr Cooper, the teacher – now she could say his name – came over to the machine. 'Patti?' And Patti came, too. But this time Patti helped Ugaso to load the disc herself, and to use the mouse to call up the page she wanted – the page about Somalia; and the picture of home, of the acacia trees and the stream.

Once more, Patti and the rest of the world disappeared for Ugaso; the sounds of the children in the library were stilled and the movements about her frozen. It was as if she was *inside* the picture, with the woman and the water pot, and the camels, and the stream, hearing the sheep and listening hard in case she might be mistaken and of them was the sound of her father laughing.

And tears ran down to salt her smile.

When she looked round to see if the others had seen the tears, they'd all gone! The library was empty, with just the hum of the computer for company. Mr Cooper had led them out, and left her to enjoy her picture of home. And she stayed there until she heard the sounds of the others out at play, when she went to catch up with them.

That night, she told her mother about the computer picture. Her mother was getting the meal, and either she didn't want to make much of it, or she was too busy.

'That was then,' her mother said. 'This is now.'

Which made Ugaso go further. 'I sometimes dream that Dad is in the picture,' she told her.

'That is stupid! Dad *was*. We three are what there is now.' And with her pestle she pounded the rice as if it were an enemy.

It was the weekend, and her mother spent the Saturday showing her which bus took them to the street market, and how to go to the post office to get money. And on the way home she said, 'Forget Dad' in the same matter-of-fact voice she'd used to buy the bus tickets.

Fridays became very special days for Ugaso; because in spite of what her mother said, she still couldn't think of London as her home. And going to the library meant that she could call up her special picture on the computer.

She started to learn some of the words on the screen, the way they were written. She could see the words for 'acacia' and 'tree' while 'Somalia' looked much the same; it was almost like *Soomaaliya*.

But on one of the days, in Library Time,

Dean Wilson came over and pushed her off the computer. 'Pillock trees!' Which Ugaso understood. She stared at his thin white face, screwed up in a trod-in-sheep-droppings look.

'London!' he said. And he grabbed the mouse, and her wrist, and forced her to stand and watch while he called up a picture of a big London clock, the one they showed on the news at night.

'Xxx Xxx,' he said proudly, and stuck out the chest of his shirt with his thumbs.'

But most library days she was left on her own with her picture; looking into it with moony eyes – although the image of her father laughing through the acacia trees grew weaker and weaker, Friday by Friday.

One night after the big clock had been on the television and the newsreader was talking, she heard the man say, 'Somalia'. Although she couldn't follow all the words she sat with her mother, both as stiff as mahogany trees, as the film showed the fighting there – those trucks packed with clansmen with guns, firing into the air and smiling at the camera.

One of the tribes had won a battle; and they didn't look like the fighters on her father's side.

Ugaso didn't sleep that night; but she didn't cry either, because her eyes couldn't make any more tears. Her fear for her father had gone past all that, deep into her bones.

The next day, the minute she was back in school, she asked to go to the library; and Mr Cooper let her. He must have seen the news as well. There was another class having Library Time, but the computer wasn't being used; so she was allowed to have it.

She called up her picture; and, sitting there, she looked at the image of her homeland until it went into a blur, and disappeared as she closed her eyes in a sort of prayer.

That night, there was a lot of shouting and wailing round the flats, with kids rocking the cars to set off their alarms. They ran when the blue flashing light of a police-car came through – but up on the seventh floor Ugaso and her mother double-bolted the door, and pushed a table against it. Who knew where those kids might have run?

And Ugaso went cold in her bed when the thumping suddenly started on their own door.

She went under the covers, and

under the pillows. So did her mother. If they ignored it, it would go away; the hooligans outside would move on to hound someone else.

But, bang, bang, bang it went. And they hadn't a telephone for calling for help.

The banging became a thumping; not knuckles now but fists. And, what was creepy, there was no calling or shouting. Just *thump, thump, thump. Come and see what's out here!* it seemed to torment.

It was like the clansmen who came in the night, with petrol and fire.

Ugaso and her mother tried to pretend it wasn't happening. But when little Ali woke and started shouting in fear, they had to do something about it. There had been a silence when they'd thought it had gone away, but then *thump, thump, thump* it had come again.

Ugaso's mother crept from the bedroom

and found a long broom. Ali was carried to the furthest corner of the kitchen, down behind a cupboard, where Ugaso picked up a vegetable knife. And while her mother stood back Ugaso crawled across the table barricade to the little spy hole.

She squinted through, ready to see the faces of hate outside.

And saw her father standing there.

Her father! Thin, tired, beard all scrawny and grey, and lost in a big overcoat – but her father, with those same father's eyes that never change.

'Aabe!' she shouted, their own word for 'Dad'.

Desperately, she and her mother pulled against each other in their haste to get the door open, fast. It thudded on Ugaso's foot, but she didn't feel it. They dragged her father in and hugged him – till they'd done him almost as much damage as the enemy fighters had.

And, in between being kissed and fed he told them how badly things had gone for their clan, how so many of the rest were dead and rotting in scrub – but how lucky he'd been to get across the border into Ethiopia, to a Red Crescent camp, and on a refugee flight to Britain.

And how, since coming to Britain, he had been a week tracking them down.

'So,' he said, looking round, 'this is where we are...'

The next day, Ugaso didn't go to school. She couldn't, in case her father wasn't there when she went home, and it had all been a dream. She stayed with him in the flat, and when he woke up, she told him all the English she had learned – and he was pleased with her.

But she went to school on the Friday, and when it was Library Time, she asked Mr Cooper, as usual, 'Please, I use the computer?'

He nodded. 'Xx xxxxxx. Do you want xx xxxx your picture of Somalia xxxxx?'

But Ugaso shook her head. 'No,' she said. 'I want today looking at a picture of London.' He frowned, and she smiled. A big smile.

'Where I live now,' she said.

STRONGER THAN SPRITE

Milly Webster danced everywhere – in
from school, out to play, up to bed –
and in her dreams. She felt the beat
in everything she heard, and she saw
whatever space she was in as a stage
she could fill with movement. Slow, fast,
smooth, twirly – her feet took the lead
and her body swayed and stretched,
curled or glided, according to the rhythm
in her head. When Mrs Hunter at school
lined up Nightingale class after play,
she never put Milly at the front because
they'd all go in doing the conga.

'She's got dancing in her blood, that
girl.'

'Or it could be the Sprite,' her father reckoned. 'She's got plenty of fizz, that's for sure.' But he was only being modest, because he knew where she got her dancing from. Her mother had been to ballet school before she grew too big, and her nan had danced in the chorus line at the London Palladium.

'Dance today!' Milly always woke early on Fridays. She needed to make sure her black leotard was packed in her school bag; but she had another reason. Her hair. On dance days she asked her mother to tie it behind her head in a bunch, like the statuette of a ballet dancer that stood on the mantelpiece: head high, back straight, short skirt, and long legs. That was her, wasn't it – at least on Fridays? Well, not *exactly*, but it was near enough – with her hair done like that it was definitely the way she felt.

Miss Bird took the lessons. The school hall was a great space to dance in; and from the beginning in the infants Milly had lived for dance days. There was no messing about, no boy was ever allowed not to hold a girl's hand, and you didn't choose partners, you were given them, and you liked it. Sometimes the music was fast, like being blown by a gust of wind; sometimes slow, like riding a cloud on a summer's day. But whatever Miss Bird did with them, Milly's imagination always seemed to give her the right feelings for the music.

As she moved up into the juniors she got to love the more disciplined dancing they did, as well as the tricky twisting and gyrating where she could go off on her own. And what she liked as well, when they practised for an assembly, was that Miss Bird always talked to them like professionals, saying 'upstage' and 'downstage', 'stage left', 'stage right', and 'out front'.

But when Milly danced out of bed that particular Friday, holding her balance on one foot in front of the long mirror and pulling back her hair, how was she to know today was going to be so special?

Miss Bird sat them all in a circle in the hall – heads high, shoulders down, backs straight, legs crossed symmetrically.

'Our school is very lucky,' she said. 'We've been chosen to take a dance troupe to the Children's Dance Festival in the town hall. In five weeks' time ...'

Milly's back had suddenly never been straighter, her nose never higher. Miss Bird was saying this for a reason.

'... And our school is going to do something different. Instead of our troupe being all Year Six children, or

Year Two, or the headmaster and Mrs Grundy' – she knew how to get a laugh – 'our group's going to be made up of children from all my junior classes, to dance a piece called *Story*. And at the end of today's lesson I shall select a girl and a boy from Nightingale to be part of that troupe. So please show me your best work.'

Milly's heart started doing a polka, and inside her head a dervish whirled. Dancing at the town hall! Wouldn't it be something if she was picked to dance on that stage? She'd seen loads of shows there, pantomimes, musicals, concerts, and a touring ballet. The main hall was all set up like a real theatre, with proper curtains, rows and rows of lights, and a stage big enough for *Swan Lake*. To be on that stage where all those professionals had danced, under the sort of spotlights

where you couldn't see the audience?
What a dream!

But would she? Could she be the girl to be chosen? No matter what Mrs Hunter said about her being a dancer, Miss Bird never treated her differently from anybody else. She encouraged everyone, she tried to see them all improving in their own ways, giving them hints to suit *them*. And that went for her. However well she'd done the last exercise, she'd always be given something else to think about; there was always 'somewhere to go'.

So, whether or not she'd be picked was all down to how well she danced today.

It was 'free dance'. 'I'm going to put on some music, I want you to listen to it through, twice, and then on the second repeat, do what the music tells you, let your heads and your feet take you on your own dance journey. And no crashes at the crossroads!'

Miss Bird clicked her iPod and the music started playing. Milly stood up straight away. She wasn't going to listen to the music sitting down – she couldn't, she wanted her whole body to hear it; of course her ears, but her brain, too, and her feet, and all the muscles she'd be using.

'*Scheherazade*,' Miss Bird said. 'Composed by Rimsky Korsakov.'

The music began loud and forceful, sort of 'listen to this!', changing to something faster and lighter with little pauses a bit like commas – before it went sweeping and twirling, jumping, even, until it spun round and round like a whirlpool, and finished very quietly, winding down into stillness.

'I've cut that to size for today,' Miss Bird said, 'in case anyone knows the piece.'

No one looked as if they did; it was definitely new to Milly. But she could feel herself really wanting to dance to it.

'Listen again.'

Milly listened again and some ideas came into her head. She looked around the hall to see where she might go in this part, that part, where she might have room for a twirl, a turn, a little jump. And by the time she'd heard it through the second time her legs were twitching to get going.

'OK, Nightingale – so let's see how you do. And enjoy it!'

Miss Bird stood ready to click her iPod again, by which time Milly had run to where she wanted to start; not in the middle of the hall but towards the back.

'And ...'

Click. *Scheherazade* started again.

For the loud and dramatic opening Milly kept her body still but threw her arms into the air, twice; and as the faster theme came in she weaved through the others, light steps punctuated by skips, and two little leaps. As the music whirled, she whirled, two movements at once – her body twisting and a wider gyration around the hall – until for the final, haunting notes she sank, dropping to the floor slowly like a leaf in autumn.

'That was very good. Some lovely work there. I only wish I could pick you all.' But Miss Bird couldn't. Milly knew it, everyone knew it.

'I'm going to tell you who I've chosen straight away, but just to say that if either of my choices can't commit themselves to the rehearsals and the night itself, then I shall have two reserves in mind. But for now I have chosen Milly Webster and Carlos Alva.'

It took a second or so to realise what Miss Bird had just said. *'Milly Webster.'* She was going to be in the school dance troupe! She was going to dance on the proper stage at the town hall! She nodded modestly, muttered thank you – and wished that the rest of the dance lesson would melt into the floor, just in case she did something stupid and Miss Bird changed her mind.

'I'll give you a letter to take home to your parents,' she told Milly and Carlos – and straight-off got on with the rest of the lesson.

Carlos Alva. Her partner was going to be Carlos Alva. He was red hot for football, was up the ropes quicker than anyone else in PE, and he was a really good dancer. He made dance look a muscly thing for boys to do, and if Miss Bird hadn't always chosen people's partners he'd have been the first to get picked by all the girls, every time. And now he was going to be her partner in the school troupe.

So ... This was going to be a really good five weeks. She couldn't wait to get home to share the letter. And she could hear what they'd say indoors. Mum would go, 'Ooooer!' and Dad would say, 'Dancing on the town hall stage! Where's it all going to end?'

As for herself – she would dance all night in her bed.

The dancers met three lunch hours a week as well as after school on Thursdays, when they went on until nearly six o'clock. There were sixteen of them, and she and Carlos were the two youngest: six from the top class, four from the next two years, and her and Carlos from Nightingale. The music wasn't easy. It was *Scheherazade* again, but for the show they would dance a ten-minute version. At their first rehearsal she played it through to them, from start to finish.

'It's a story of dark and light. It's called *The Thousand and One Nights* – wicked and cruel, about a rich and powerful sultan, that's like a king, who is badly betrayed by his wife; so he takes revenge on all women by marrying a princess every night and killing her the next morning ...'

'The dirty dog!'

'... Night after night, morning after morning, the gruesome business goes on. *Until!*' Miss Bird sat them up with a change of voice. 'Young Princess

Scheherazade from the sultan's court volunteers to be his next bride. She has a plan! And at bedtime she starts to tell him a story that lasts all night through, until he's so caught up in it that when dawn breaks, he just *has* to know what happens next ...'

'Like a good book,' one of the older girls said, piously.

'... So he spares her. And the next night Scheherazade finishes that first story and starts straight off on another, making sure there's still more to tell when the sun comes up. She's spared again – and she goes on and on like this, finishing one tale, beginning another, for a thousand and one nights ...'

'Longer than *Corrie*.'

'... At the end of which, the sultan has fallen in love with Scheherazade and her stories, and he makes her his queen.'

'A beginning, a middle, and a happy ending,' one of the boys reckoned.

'But a man having that power over women is nothing to celebrate. What comes from *The Thousand and One Nights* is the power of story itself – in spoken words, books, art, and music. The triumph of *story* is what it celebrates. And in our dance the older boys will be sultans, the older girls will be Scheherazades telling stories, and the younger dancers will be the stories themselves, worked out between partners and weaving in and out of the action.'

Milly was ready to stand up and get on with it. She wanted to hear that music again and to start moving to it, get something going with Carlos – because an idea had come into her head. *Aladdin*. She'd seen the pantomime at the town hall, she could remember the funny stuff, the songs – but mostly the dancing boys and girls twisting and swirling to music a bit like *Scheherazade*. So what about her being Aladdin, finding the magic lamp and being chased for it by Carlos as Abanazar the wicked uncle? One scene in the market place had been terrific, where all the traders' stalls had been tipped over in the chase, the stage filled with streaming silks and coloured birds let out of cages.

The music played again, and she and Carlos talked, both limbering up, trotting on the spot, bending and stretching. She told him her idea.

'I like that,' he said, 'being the wicked uncle, chasing you for the magic lamp ...'

'Stuff would get knocked over, pots roll ...' Milly was thinking of some leaps she could do to the music.

'And you're dodging the people as you try to escape from your wicked uncle. "Ah – ha-ha-ha-ha-ha!" ' He was getting into character already.

Around the hall all the others were talking or moving, some laughing, some head-scratching; with Miss Bird coming to them and listening to ideas and possibilities.

'That sounds a good starting point,' she told Milly and Carlos. 'And the Aladdin story actually was in *The Thousand and One Nights*. Well done! See where you go with it.'

She moved on, and while the music played over again, she took her top class sultans and princesses to one side to begin teaching them the more formal choreography.

After a while they put it all together, to see how things fitted; and after a couple of runs-through, and stopping, and going again, it all began to fall into place. And the great thing for Milly was that their story-dance, hers and Carlos's, fitted in well with plenty of dramatic moments where she was almost caught, flitting off around the market stalls, holding the imaginary lamp aloft.

But the really exciting bit was going to come at the end. Miss Bird called them together again.

'Now, everyone will be in black vests and leggings and bare feet throughout – the theatre will have a stage-cloth down. But on top, the sultans will wear turbans, and the princesses will wear baggy Arabian trousers. For the finale, though, all the different stories become *the* story. So, as you come off, *all* the boys put on turbans, and *all* the girls pull on trousers over their leggings. Everyone is the sultan, and everyone is Princess Scheherazade; then, for a final tableau as the music fades, one sultan and one princess will dance themselves into a position to pose in a spotlight, centre-stage. And our two youngest dancers – representing all the stories in the world yet to come – will pose on either side of them.'

This was going to be fantastic! Milly and Carlos were those youngest dancers.

Miss Bird told them how the sultan would bow to Scheherazade, and she, Paula Prentice – a girl who went to proper ballet lessons – would go up on 'points' in her ballet shoes, and hold her position with her head in the air and her arms raised as the music played out and the spotlight slowly faded. 'If you can do it, let's use it!' – and Paula Prentice could. But the great thing was, Miss Bird wanted

Milly and Carlos to be the pair on either side, sharing that spotlight.

'Not on points, Milly – on the balls of your feet – but copying Scheherazade in all other aspects.'

They practised it, and actually, Milly found it easy, her only problem being that she was puffed out by then and had to look as if she wasn't. But she knew it was going to look good. And wouldn't her mum and dad be proud? Her in a spotlight on the town hall stage!

From then on it was hard work, tough going. And – when Milly thought about it afterwards – that session was probably the easiest of all, before the dance was more or less fixed and everyone had to concentrate on the repetition and the discipline of doing it the same way, the same, the same, the same, every time. But, 'Coming along!' Miss Bird would say at the end of a rehearsal; sending them all away uplifted.

Gradually, the different pieces gelled together. The main theme was the sultans being put in different moods by the princesses as they danced and mimed the telling of their stories; but the minor theme was the younger dancers weaving their own stories in and out to the music.

And so they practised. As Aladdin, Milly escaped the grasping hands of Carlos's wicked uncle, ducking, stretching, leaping – all fitting-in well with the others – until Miss Bird suddenly came up with a new idea. A very difficult idea, and she said she wasn't sure if Milly would be able to do it. 'But it'll be cracking if you can.'

'What, Miss?'

'I'd like you to try a proper pirouette.'

'A pirouette?' Milly had heard the word.

'A ballet twist of the body, spinning on one foot, arms horizontal. A full turn, fast round and finishing balanced. And that's the hard part, not wobbling at the end.' Miss Bird demonstrated how it was done.

Milly tried one – but she didn't get all the way around and ended up facing the side. The next time, she got all the way around, but she did wobble and had to put a foot out to steady herself.

'It'll be marvellous if it works. Abanazar has trapped you and goes to throw his arms round you, but you take him by surprise and pirouette, holding it for that vital beat before you slide free.'

Milly nodded her head. It would be good if she could do it, because no one else – not even the dancers in the top class – had been asked to do a pirouette.

She tried one more, and it was a bit better.

'Let's run it, check that it fits.' Miss Bird clapped her hands. 'From where you come round downstage, when Abanazar gets closest to grabbing you ...'

'Near the snake charmer blowing his pipe ...' Milly could see it all in her head.

'Whatever. Let him reach you, and his touch spins you, sets you off on your pirouette. Which baffles him for a second – and then you're away, out of his clutches.'

Milly nodded.

'But you must finish still and upright for a full count of one or it'll look messy.'

Milly understood. It was the same in gymnastics if you tottered at the end of a sequence. It spoiled everything you'd just done.

'OK? And ...' Miss Bird clapped them

through it. Carlos came running around the centre of the floor, reached out at Milly, and this time she spun into her pirouette – a dizzy turn, head round fast, arms horizontal, and stood balanced for a full beat. Which wasn't bad.

'Not easy. But practise! Practise! You'll be downstage-left in a good light – it'll look very effective. We'll see how we go.'

Milly and Carlos found space of their own and tried the touch and the pirouette a couple more times. And it worked sometimes, and sometimes not quite. This was definitely not going to be easy, and Carlos made a suggestion. 'We'll do it the old way, and the new way, so we're up for both if you think you've got the wobbles on the day.'

Milly gave him a look. 'Thanks for that!' And just for him she did a perfect pirouette, except as she finished, beautifully balanced, he seemed to be looking somewhere else. She blew out her cheeks. Dance had been natural to her before, that's what they said – she was a born dancer. And up to now, that's what she'd been doing in lessons and practises – dancing naturally. But right now, at this rehearsal, she realised that a real dancer isn't just born, they're made, too: helped, told things, developed, got better; and probably shouted at sometimes when things went wrong. And they practised, practised, practised, to get the difficult bits right.

And that's what she was going to do. Practise. And find out what sort of dancer she really was.

She worked hard with Carlos, not just at the pirouette but all through the dance. Meanwhile, everywhere else in her life she pirouetted: in her garden, in her bedroom, outside on the pavement, and going down to the shop. She practised and practised; and gradually the pirouette worked a lot more often than it didn't. She looked at pirouettes on the internet at home, and even worked out a private routine to help her practise, where she pirouetted and stood, pirouetted and stood, pirouetted and stood, made it into a little sequence of three in a row, just for fun.

In the week of the show they did a rehearsal on the town hall stage. Each school was given a couple of hours. And it was different from the start. In the school hall Milly had imagined she was running offstage with plenty of space to go into; but here, up on the proper stage, she was in the wings for real and nearly running into a brick wall. And there was a surprise, even for Miss Bird, who was cross with herself and said she should have known. The stage had a slope, from the back wall down to the footlights.

'It's raked! It's called a "rake". But I've seen worse. It gives a better view for the audience in the stalls, enables upstage performers to be seen. So we just have to get used to it.'

They all did, mucking about at first as if they were on a ship's deck in a stormy sea. Laughing with them, Miss Bird finally clapped her hands, told them to take up beginners' positions for a run-through, and went down the apron steps to stand in the middle of the stalls.

'Cue music!' she called.

Milly and Carlos stood in the wings in their starting positions upstage left, waiting for their first entrance – watching the opening. The run-through began.

And now Milly's heart wasn't her own, it belonged to a humming bird keeping time with its wings; and her legs felt as strong as two damp straws.

The sultan's theme came in, loud, frightening – replied to by the Scheherazade violin, up and down; and as the music rose and fell, Milly danced onstage, into her mind's eye of a market place, round and round, offstage and on again, her body avoiding the other dancers and her imagination taking her in and out of the stalls in her Arabian market, past the snake charmer, and under the perches of exotic birds.

It was hard for them all. There were some collisions, the rake threw some dancers off-balance, but Miss Bird let the music run until it came to Milly's big moment. She stood puffed and panting in the wings waiting for her entrance for the pirouette. And, finally, here came her cue. On she danced, Carlos behind her, reaching, grabbing, never quite making it. She did one of her little leaps, twisted upstage and down, and ran across the front towards the footlights where she would almost be caught. And as she felt Carlos's hand brushing her arm she went into her pirouette – take off, fast twist all the way around, arms wide and straight, and finished standing still, with just a slight wobble. No, a definite wobble. But she held it for a beat, and danced off ready for the final section where Scheherazade is spared by the sultan, and goes into the final tableau, up on points, with Milly holding the same pose. The end.

'And … curtain!' Miss Bird called – although there wasn't one, not this evening.

They all sat on the stage, flushed and perspiring.

'That wasn't bad for a first run. A few near collisions, a bit too much *thinking* going on, but that's not a bad thing with four days still to go. You coped with the rake fairly well, that won't be a problem, and I saw some lovely pieces of work...'

What about Carlos and me? Milly thought. She was pleased it was good over-all, but what about that pirouette? She'd very nearly made it, hadn't she?

Miss Bird talked to the whole troupe before going round to pairs and to individuals – and at last she came to Milly and Carlos.

'Some lovely work,' she said. 'I felt Aladdin's panic, and I knew Abanazar's greed. You interpreted the music beautifully, perhaps a bit rushed in the beginning, Carlos – you nearly *had*

to catch Aladdin, didn't you? But – '
And here she looked at Milly. *Did there
always have to be a 'but'?* 'I think we'll
lose the pirouette. It's chancy. It's been
good eight, nine times out of ten, but
we must be able to rely on it – no
possible chance of a wobble, no extra
step however small, or the whole effect
will be ruined.' She smiled. 'It's still all
very good, though, and very telling. Well
done!' And she moved on to speak to
somebody else.

Milly looked down at the black stage-
cloth, and through a mizzle of tears
she traced her fingers along a small
crease in it, down a little pathway of
disappointment. *Not do the pirouette!* She'd
worked at it, and worked at it, she'd
pirouetted everywhere – and now she
wouldn't be doing it on the night. What
a pity Miss Bird had thought of it in the

first place – then she wouldn't have felt such a failure.

'Never mind,' Carlos said. 'It's ace as it is.'

But nothing should ever be ace as it was! Everything should get a bit better. Ten times out of ten by Saturday; she knew she'd have done it. But not now, she wasn't going to get the chance to go for a perfect pirouette.

And that really was a rotten feeling.

It came. The big night. For five weeks Milly had lain in bed looking up at that ceiling and seeing pictures of the Scheherazade dance. And now she was going to do it for real. At school that week they'd run it and run it; and for all the reasons she'd felt good about being chosen, she was feeling good about things again; the town hall stage; her family being there;

partnering Carlos. Pirouette or not, tonight was going to be a night to remember.

The dancers met Miss Bird at the school and went to the town hall in the minibus. Milly's parents already had their tickets and were making their own way there. 'Make us proud,' Dad said. 'Break a leg!' said Mum. And they all knew not to say 'good luck'.

However professional the stage might have been, the town hall wasn't a real theatre – so the dancers didn't have to be squeezed into backstage dressing rooms, and nobody was going to have to keep shushing them all the time. There was a large conference room beneath the main hall, which for tonight was divided by screens into dressing areas for all eight schools in the festival. As Milly and her troupe arrived the atmosphere down there fizzed like static electricity. The place smelt like a gym, a hairdresser's, a treatment room, and twenty perfume counters, all sprayed into one. Dance costumes were laid out on chairs, props were organised on tables, and people jigged about as if they were dying to go to the loo.

'Everything's set, we're in block H in the balcony, and we shall all go up there together.' The theatre balcony was reserved for the performers, which meant they could see some of the others dancing before being called out school by school in the intervals between pieces. 'We're on number six, and we'll get our call two dances before, which gives good time for a warm-up.' Miss Bird seemed nervous to Milly. Well, she thought, it might be a *festival* and not a *competition*, but she bet the teachers all wanted theirs to be better than any of the others.

And Milly was pretty certain theirs would be. Not many schools would have a dance teacher like Miss Bird.

The time hung in the air like an airship going over, then it started flying like a jet out of London City Airport. And now here they were, her and Carlos sitting next to one another in block H of the balcony, their knees jiggling nervously as the lights went down and the curtain rose on the first school to perform. It was a good opener – a modern jazz dance to a ripping electric soundtrack that really got the place going. It had people in the audience standing and whooping at the end – and Milly thinking how different their dance would be with its whirly, twirly, Arabian music. How would that go down? Well, that's what they were going to do, so she'd just have to hope people liked it.

A folk dance followed, then a 'movement' piece more like gymnastics, then a ballet school item – and while the audience applauded at the end of that, Miss Bird gave block H the nod and led them down to the conference room to change and warm-up – ready for *Story*, danced to *Scheherazade* by Rimsky Korsikov. They had created it, they had practised it, they had rehearsed it for five weeks. Now they would go out onto that stage and perform it.

In the wings Milly was all jangly nerves as the school before them took their curtain call. The stage went dark and the others ran off – one of their dancers forgetting the rake and taking a tumble in the confusion – and on ran Milly's troupe into their starting positions, Milly and Carlos in the wings stage-left. The audience went quiet, and up went the curtain on *Story*, the spots and floods filling the stage with warm Arabian light.

From the big town hall amps came the opening chords of the strong sultan theme, then the fluttering violin for Princess Sheherazade, and – counting the beats – on danced Milly as Aladdin. She found the imaginary magic lamp and played with it, she rubbed it and a genii came out; but Carlos as Abanazar saw it and started to chase. She skipped and dodged, knew every step and every move so well she didn't have to think about them. She flitted, darted, twisted and leapt. She curled, stretched and swayed. Her hair shone, her face glowed, her body sang with the joy of the dance. And it felt good.

The dance went on. In her exits into the wings Milly saw Miss Bird, congratulating, encouraging, big eyes and a wide smile, her head held high, peering out at every inch of that stage.

'Marvellous! Marvellous!' she mouthed.

Until near the end when the accident happened.

All the sultans and princesses were in their turbans and baggy trousers, so were all the 'stories'. Milly could see the special spotlight following the principal sultan and Scheherazade around the stage, growing brighter and tighter as the climax came nearer. But suddenly, on an upstage run when she was ready to turn and face the sultan, Paula Prentice's ballet shoes with their blocked toes caught in the stage-cloth where it had been rucked. Miraculously she kept some sort of shape as she dived and fell offstage, but Milly could see she wasn't going to get up quickly. Miss Bird was there, stooping to her, then gesturing frantically for one of the other princesses to take her place. There was the sultan looking lost on his own – and Miss Bird's voice hissing, 'Sonya! Sonya! Take over for Paula!' But Sonya didn't; she'd nearly gone over the same ruck herself and was staying where she normally was, pretending not to hear. Everyone just kept doing what they always did.

And here came the sultan, down towards the front, still in the white 'follow spot', dancing as if Scheherazade was there – but she wasn't. And it did look odd. It looked all wrong, not symmetrical the way Miss Bird had wanted things. And this was the finale!

What would happen? Would the teacher come on and stop the dance?

Please, no! Not that. It had been good right up to then; it was just that the ending would look a bit odd.

But why should it? Couldn't something be done, by someone?

A sudden surge filled Milly, a fizz inside like shaken-up Sprite. *She* would do something! She was in the right place. But, *what?* What could she do? There were too many beats to go before she could take up her balls-of-the-feet pose. She had to fill in with something until the music wound down, although she didn't know what that could be. But as she danced into the spotlight with the sultan the fierce blinding brightness suddenly seemed to tell her to do something – and taking a deep breath she took her chance, went for it. She threw herself into a pirouette, a fast twist, arms wide and horizontal, head round fast, and hold for a beat. No wobble! But that hadn't taken long enough, so she went again, and then again. As the music played out she pirouetted all the way around the Sultan, as if a young Scheherazade was dancing rings round him. Not every pirouette was perfect, but as near as made no difference in this emergency. Finally, she went up onto the balls of her feet in the final pose she had rehearsed; and so the music faded, and the spot went out.

Down came the curtain – to a loud whooping and clapping up there on the stage, never mind the auditorium.

Carlos kissed her cheek but Milly was too flushed with success to really notice. No feeling could ever be as fantastic as this.

'Thank you!' Miss Bird was there, hugging her. 'You saved us at the end! Such *professional* thinking.'

Milly looked up at her. 'It just, sort of, came to me. I had to do something in that light. So I took a chance.'

'You are a star!'

Milly's chest rose with pride.

'But another time, the right arm, second into the pirouette – remember, horizontal and straight, always horizontal and straight. Arms do tend to droop when the head's facing the other way.'

Milly nodded. 'Yes, Miss.'

And at that moment, as they were hurried off the stage for the stage-cloth ruck to be sorted and the next school to come on, Milly knew that one day she was going to be a professional dancer. It was in her blood, it was in her bones, it was in her head – and a lot stronger than Sprite.

SALLY CINDERELLA

1

Sally never seemed right, never looked
up to very much. Some people have the
knack of looking good all the time –
every day Queen of the May. They might
be dressed in old clothes and climbing
out of a pig sty but they somehow
sparkle and smile, their eyes come
through, and you can always take a photo
you'd like to keep. Handsome. Pretty.
Really up to the mark.

But others could spend a year in front
of a mirror and still wouldn't get a stare

from a cat. Perhaps it all comes from inside: and there are some people who feel so miserable most of the time they don't care whether they're walking to a party – or off the nearest bridge. And Sally Lane knew more about pavements than she did about the sky, knew tree roots better than the leaves. A smile for her would have worked muscles that hurt. It wasn't the same for her sisters – it wasn't the same for the dog – but that's how it was for Sally.

She was up and dressed and down at the shop before most of the others had opened their eyes.

'Lottery,' her mother said one morning, 'an' sugar.' She gave her no money, just pressed her pencil message into a soft piece of cardboard: soft looking numbers and words, hard heart, because her mother know that certain stupid people felt sorry for Sally Lane. She was always the one to send when she wasn't going to pay.

Mrs Vasisht was one of them: and so was Kompel, who helped in the shop when she wasn't at school. Sally was only six but everyone seemed to know her.

'Yeah?' Kompel asked as the thin little girl slid in round the door.

Sally gave up the note, her eyes as usual on the floor. Kompel took it gently – because she knew a quick moving arm would make her flinch.

'Hang on. I'll have to ask.'

Sally waited. She was used to this. Not paying usually meant a bit of fuss. She yawned, eyed the fresh bread, smelt its heat.

'Sorry, tell your mother not lottery.' Mrs Vasisht had come out. 'Sugar OK, but not lottery.' She waved her fingers in a 'no' sign. 'Lottery only for grown ups. Little children not allowed to play.' The

shopkeeper's face was unsmiling, but
then she was unsmiling with everyone,
she wasn't picking on Sally.

Kompel gave Sally the smallest packet
of sugar on the shelf. 'It's the law, Sal,' she
explained. 'See? My mum and dad gets into
trouble if they let kids do the lottery ...'

Sally stared at her, took back the cardboard note with *lottery* crossed through,
walked out of the shop. She sighed as she
went and her steps were slower than they
had, been coming. Slower steps, faster
heart – because going home without the
full message meant she'd done wrong.
And doing wrong always got her a good
hiding ...

2

Kompel may have been hard worked, but
she had never been hard hit. Working

hard in the shop was natural, was expected. You didn't sit and watch much telly when your dad was stuck behind a Post Office grille all day and only came out on short visits. Everyone in the family worked. Even little Sunil had to carry cola bottles and jump his frail weight on cardboard boxes.

But no one ever got hit. Dad might hold your hand hard, or look at you that sad way. But hard hitting was for ants, and beetles, and mice. And the only other sort was for backs, soft pats, when people were please with you.

Kompel worked hard in school, too. She was good at maths because maths was what she *had* to know. Weights and litres and money– checking the red numbers on the till, getting the change correct. And that helped to make school a good place to go. To get things right, to draw and dance and write poetry: all of which came from inside, from the energy of the sun that seemed to shine within her.

On the morning of the lottery Kompel got to the playground just before the bell, didn't have time for a game with anyone. But she did see Sally Lane, standing on her own over by the kitchen – watching her sisters playing chase.

Kompel shrugged. *No lottery* wasn't down to her, was it? She couldn't make everything right for Sally. And she definitely couldn't make Sally's sisters play with her.

The bell was just about to go – and so was Kompel, when Sally stared over at her and suddenly twisted herself away again. A sort of, *'You!'* look. *'You!'*

Well, it wasn't my fault! Kompel told herself. I'm sorry – but I didn't make the law about selling lottery tickets. All the same, it had annoyed her, little Sally's huff. She felt *sorry* for her, she didn't deserve that sort of look.

The first bell went, and most people stopped. Then the second, and they started going in.

Sally pulled herself off her wall and came towards Kompel. And Kompel, a monitor and expected in last, stood there and stared at her.

What was that? Sally looked different somehow, even to this morning. She wasn't the same as when she'd come into the shop before school. Not quite. Something was different about her. Around the face.

Her cheek was swollen. She'd got a red, fiery mark under her eye, and she'd been crying.

'What's up, Sal? What've you done?'

But Sally barely gave Kompel the time for an answer. She hurried on past, her eyes on the grey of the ground. 'Door swang back,' she said.

And that was all. No being cross with the door, the way people are.

And definitely no details.

3

Kompel had another good day. She was in on a few laughs, wrote a long piece about the month of May, won at volley-ball. She should have gone home happy. But somehow she didn't, couldn't – and Sally Lane was the cause of that. Her bad face had stayed with Kompel all day.

Poor little kid, she thought, being sent to school like that. No ointment on her face. No plaster. Not seen to, probably, because they were cross with her over going home without doing the lottery. By playtime one of the helpers gave her cream to put on it, but that wasn't the same as having her mum or her dad look after her, was it?

Kompel got home and turned-to in the shop. They were always busy with kids after school, buying penny chews and picture cards. You needed eyes everywhere, more like being a teacher than a shop keeper. But, as her mum said, don't look down your nose at it. It was all the cheap bits, the small packets which kept the corner shop going. They all went to *Asda* for their big stuff; and came here for what was handy. And for the slate, when they wanted tick.

The 'slate' was the book where Kompel's mother wrote what people owed. People with regular business at the Post Office counter could run up little bills – then on benefits day they had to settle.

And being Thursday, Mrs Lane came in for the Post Office, after the main rush.

No one could tell how hard she was on Sally, not by looking at her. She seemed an ordinary sort of person, not some cruel witch. She'd got little Lindy with her, and she bought her a Twix, stroking the kid's white-blonde hair.

'Sorry about lottery,' Kompel's mother said. 'We're having to be very careful right now.'

'Oh, that's all right, love. Do it now. Never know your luck, do you, Lind?'

Lindy shook her head as if it were a known fact, like those you learned in school. Important.

If you asked her, Kompel couldn't tell what made her say what she did. All she knew was that she suddenly heard herself saying it.

'Shame about Sally's face.'

Mrs Lane turned and stared at her, cold. It was like looking into the face of some dangerous animal which might suddenly spring, and bite you.

'Yeah!' she said. 'Clumsy little cat, weren't she, Lind? Fell down the steps.'

Lindy nodded: didn't bat an eye.

Mrs Lane's voice was flat and freezing. Lindy's eyes were like ice. But the real chill was in Kompel's stomach.

Falling down the steps wasn't what Sally had said. *'Door swang back,'* had been her words. Different stories. And neither of them was the truth, Kompel guessed. Because to be honest with herself, she'd known all day, hadn't she? Little Sally Lane hadn't had an accident. She'd been punched, like an enemy.

4

'You don't get involved in all that,'
Kompel's mother told her late that night.
And her father made that clicking noise
in his throat which said he agreed with
her. 'It's bad business to tell tales on
customers. People soon stop coming in if
they think we're secret police.'

Three sentences, quickly spoken: but
adding up to a terrible moment for
Kompel: one she'd probably remember all
her life. She'd remember the meal they'd
just had and where all the things were
on the table. Because it was the first time
that she knew her parents were in the
wrong, putting the family in front of what
was right.

'How do you think it looks, eh, if we
report on them for cruelty, for this child
abuse? How long before a brick comes

through that window?' Her father's eyes seemed bigger than ever, his own skin more pale from the long days in his Post Office cell.

'An' how do you think it feels to have a punch in the face-and no one cares?' Kompel had never answered him back before. 'She's a little kid – she's six!'

'The school will know. They don't shut their eyes to things like that.'

'Not like you do, you mean!' Kompel got up and ran to her room. Angry. Crying. But leaving a long silence behind her which said they knew she was right.

5

The bruise on Sally's face got better, and quite quickly – almost as if the stares which Kompel gave her were some sort of ointment. And looking, smiling, saying

something nice was all Kompel could do
not to feel helpless.

She would have liked to do more, but
there wasn't really the chance. She would
have liked to make sure Sally never
went home without her full message,
for a start. She would have liked to talk
to Sally about that bruise, if ever she
could find a way, just to let her know
that someone cared. And about the rest
of it all. Kompel had never seen anyone
who looked so unhappy all the time, in
among a family of kids who laughed
and played and looked all right. Out at
play in Clipper Street, up at the top end
where the cars couldn't go, they'd all be
there with the others. But Sally would be
talking to a wall or crouching to an ant,
out of it, silent, while the rest made more
noise than a treeful of starlings.

'Here, what's up with Sally?' Kompel

asked her little brother Bobby, who was still fat with paddi-pants and too young not to talk. 'She a naughty girl indoors?'

'Naughty!' he nodded his head fiercely. 'Won't go a-sleep. Nick the biscuits.' His little face was overtaken with the horror of it, and the hatred.

'Oh.' Kompel pretended to understand. Then, in a low voice so that his sisters wouldn't hear. 'Gets smacks, does she?'

Little Bobby looked at her: his lips went all stiff with the seriousness of Sally having to be smacked all the time for being naughty. And he suddenly turned and toddled away as if the family silence about smacks was something he'd just that second understood.

6

From now on Kompel had an aim in life.

To make Sally Lane smile. It wasn't a great aim, not a changing-the-world sort of thing, not even a medium aim like swapping Sally's family for a nicer one. But just this small aim of changing the look on Sally's face for a second or two.

She gave the girl sweets. She found a packet of picture cards with the wrapper torn and took them to school for her. She tried to get her into a game. But it was somehow as if Sally suspected that Kompel was trying to unlock her secret – as if she was scared of something worse which might happen if she did. And she wouldn't give an inch: not a millimetre of a smile. She took what was given to her and went back inside herself, staring at the lower half of the world with eyes which never shone.

In the classroom, though, where Kompel didn't see her, Sally played a clever game. She behaved more like the rest: she answered a few questions, read her reading book, played with the dolls when she got the chance. (And smacked them a lot for being naughty.) She was like someone who didn't want to stand out – except still she never smiled.

Kompel got nowhere near achieving her aim. Worse, one morning she really let Sally down. She switched off her alarm and turned over in bed. And was cross with herself when she found out that Sally had been into the shop.

'Mrs Lane, she skipped out pretty quick yesterday. Didn't settle up. And this morning she sends for a list as long as you like. No money again! All on the slate!'

'Who came?'

'That one. Little Sally.'

'What did you do?'

'I gave her cornflakes and milk for the breakfast. For the children. But I told her, send her mother in to see me for the rest.'

Kompel kept her mouth shut tight, didn't make a row again. But she knew inside that Mrs Lane would not be happy with the message Sally had to give her. And if she hadn't turned over in bed, perhaps she could have walked home with the girl and given it instead.

7

It went on to be a very hot day: like being on the equator. The first really hot day of the year in school and it was cotton dresses on, tee-shirts off and pushing for drinks at the water taps. The cooks came in moaning about the heat as if they'd been putting up with it for weeks. And

Mr Ransom drove his car in slowly with the top down ...

In all of which Sally Lane wore a long-sleeved woolly cardigan. The rest of London was fanning itself in the hot still air and Sally Lane was dressed for the cold.

'You all right, Sal?' Kompel looked hard at the girl's face. But Sally's eyes said she couldn't trust her kindness: she couldn't afford to let anyone feel sorry for her. She stared back at Kompel, and walked away.

'I only asked!' Kompel exploded. And then felt sorry. Didn't Sally get enough of the rough end of tongues?

It was one of those days that could have been bad tempered all round. In Assembly all the windows had to be open and London came roaring in. The push, push, push of the traffic, the throaty drone of the aircraft coming in to land at Heathrow. It was too hot to sing very well, and the announcements were given in the gaps between the heavy lorries. It would have been in and straight out except for one thing. Infants' May Day, coming up the week before half term: dancing round the May Pole and crowning the Queen of the May. And today the names came out of the hat. The May Queen and the May Prince, chosen by chance from the Infants' top class.

Mrs Peters was there with two cardboard boxes. A big Q marked the Queen box, a big P the Prince.

The juniors were hot and bored, but this was a big moment for the thirty top infants, and everyone was shushed to sit ready to clap the lucky two. Kompel remembered. It would be a big day for them when it came. The procession, the crowning, the local paper with the big

camera and all the parents with theirs. A
day of being special, of fame. She hadn't
had it herself, but she could remember
the thrill of it for Wendy Dorsett, whose
smile hadn't gone off her face for a week.

'So who are the two lucky ones going
to be?' Mrs Peters was asking. 'Well,
today we're going to find out!'

Twenty-nine straight backs, twenty-nine
bright faces with tight smiles. And Sally
Lane, hunched in her cardigan, sucking
her thumb.

Everyone waited.

'And in Clipper Primary School
tradition we'll ask two year six leavers to
pull out the names. A big boy and a big
girl,' she explained for the infants. 'Let's
see now ...' Mrs Peters squinted to the
back of the hall for a couple of good faces.
'John Lunn ... and ... Kompel Vasisht.'

With heavy sighs of responsibility

John and Kompel pulled themselves up and stepped over to the front. And even something like that got Kompel's heart beating, even in her own school. All the eyes! But in a couple of minutes she was going to find her heart beating a lot harder still …

8

John Lunn was efficiency itself. When your father was a river pilot and your mother was a teacher you didn't need too much telling how to do these things. In went his hand and out came, 'Sullaiman Shamime' – said very confidently.

'Thank you, John.'

Two hundred heads craned and twisted to find Sullaiman – who was the one infant suddenly interested in the velcro on his trainers.

'So Sullaiman's our May Prince this year. And …' Mrs Peters smiled all round, and she nodded at Kompel. The hall seemed very hot now.

Kompel's fingers dipped into the box Mrs Peters was holding above her. And it was in a sudden pounding that her heart knew what her head was going to do. It went all swimrny as she did it, as she tried to make everything up to Sally Lane, to bring the ghost of a smile to her sad face, just for a second. As Kompel's hand came out of the box she saw her, the hunched-over kid who thought she was no part of anything like this.

Chelsea Knowles was the name written on the paper in beautiful italic. And *Sally Lane* was the name Kompel read out – with hardly a falter, nearly as well as John Lunn had done.

It was as if she'd pressed a small button, a faint-sounding buzzer going off in the hall. Teachers looked at one another and said things with their eyes. The other Lane children looked as if they'd drunk nasty medicine. Someone coughed.

And Mrs Peters, in that electric moment, asked to see the piece of paper. 'May I?' she said, in the voice she used when she was checking work you'd marked yourself.

Looking away, Kompel gave the paper to her. She had to give it, there was no alternative – she was like a prisoner who had to stand up straight in court while the damning evidence was read. She'd been so stupid! Why had she let herself get carried away? She had always been trusted, the teachers liked her, and the little kids thought she was grown up, what with the shop and everything.

And now she was going to look like the biggest cheat going.

Mrs Peters read the name on the paper to herself. She stared at Kompel. And she straight away said, 'Thank you, Kompel. And well done, Sally, you'll make a good May Queen.' She screwed the paper into her pocket and started the clapping – a movement of the air in the hall coming just soon enough to stop Kompel from fainting.

And still Sally didn't smile. She just stared up at Kompel and sucked harder on her thumb.

9

There was no inquest over it. No more was said. Perhaps Mrs Peters didn't know how to deal with such a thing – Kompel showing everyone how she felt about little Sally. One thing was certain: Kompel was sure the other teachers never knew. No one ever looked at her any differently for pulling that name from the hat.

Each class teacher was organising their own different dance for the day. Mrs Gullivar was seeing to the Prince and his crown and robes. And Mrs MacKay, the deputy head, was in charge of the costume for the Queen – the dress for Sally to wear.

'I'll see how it fits,' she said. Every year there were alterations to be made. The crown never needed to fit any better than the real Queen's, crowns just need careful balancing, but the dress had to be up to the mark.

Mrs Walker pulled a snobby face. 'Uggh! I don't know how you can bear to touch that child!' She drove in from Kent each day to teach at Clipper Primary. 'I'd be washing my hands for a week!'

Mrs MacKay half ignored her. 'Oh, she's not so bad, poor little devil,' she said, only her blotchy neck showing her anger.

Sally Lane had been kept behind in her classroom. Sullaiman Shamime was finished and gone, his Prince's robes hanging up like a giant puppet.

'Now then, let's see …' Mrs MacKay held the shiny pink dress up to Sally. 'Stand up straight, love.'

Sally looked at her warily, some great fear behind her eyes.

'Looks all right for length. Perhaps we'll turn the hem just half an inch.' The hem went up and down regularly, had as many needle holes as it had material. 'Now, do we need a tuck in the back?' Mrs MacKay could have been talking to some forlorn little statue. 'I hope you'll

give us a May Queen's smile on the day,
eh? Mummy *will* be pleased.' But it was
just words. They both knew the game
that was being played pretend, pretend,
pretend. 'Now, cardy off – we shan't have
that on, on the day...'

But now the statue moved. Sally drew
back, resisted, and spoke. 'Mustn't,'
she said. 'My mum told me.' She was
gripping the bottoms of the cardigan arms
with her small, chewed fingers. 'I got a
cold.'

'Oh, come on. It's a lovely hot day. I'll
take the blame.' And like the firm mother
she was herself, Mrs MacKay had the
cardigan off. 'One, two, three!'

While *four* and all the way to twenty
was silent at the sight of Sally's arm.
Where a bite, a red and white human
bite, told its own terrible story.

'How did this happen?' Mrs Peters asked her kindly, in her room. 'Who did this to you?'

Sally Lane stared sullenly at the floor.

'Eh?' the headteacher asked, as if Sally had answered and she just hadn't heard. 'Sally – how did this happen?' She waited, patiently, with just the raising of her eyebrows.

There was a long, long wait.

'Come on!' she said, just a bit more sharply.

'King,' Sally murmured. 'Our dog.'

'Oh, King! But his mouth's not this shape, is it? A dog's mouth is different altogether. Lovie, I can see the tooth marks ...'

'Didn't anyone treat it?' Mrs Mackay asked. 'No *Savlon*?' She dropped her voice. 'And what about your bad face the other day?'

But Sally was back to staring. They knew. Her eyes, suddenly sharp, said it all. The game was up – her mum's and dad's game – but she didn't want to get worse done to her for saying …

'This is a … person's … bite, Sally. And a big person's. Now, who was it? We've got to know, you'll have to tell someone …'

No amount of cajoling or explaining got another word out of her, though. No amount of being made to feel safe. No amount of telling how the school *had* to ring Social Services, and how Social Services *had* to look into it. Sally clammed right up, as if being forgiven for not telling was the last little thread of hope she had to hold on to.

11

The woman from Social Services was very kind – Ms Partridge, to be called Penny. She came quickly and she took Sally home to her parents. She showed them Sally's bad arm; and, very quietly, she wanted to know how it had happened.

The children were sent to play out at the back, and in a calm, friendly, firm way she let them know what the score was. What her powers were. How her office knew where she was and how they needn't bother shouting or abusing or threatening. All they had to do was tell her.

She made it clear that Sally herself had said nothing, except to blame the dog: but that no one had believed that, and they certainly wouldn't when a doctor took a look at that arm. She also set the school's part of it straight: they hadn't poked or pried, it was all over the May Queen, as simple as that.

'May Queen!' Brian Lane suddenly broke his fierce silence. 'Ain't they s'posed to *teach* 'em? May Queen!' He looked as if he had a lot more shout in him, too, but his wife gave him a look and he shut up, leaving his leg dangling over the arm chair to show whose house it was.

Very matter of fact, puffing smoke, Sally's mother went through different stories of the bite. The dog, it *must* have been: Sally often annoyed him, which is why she hadn't shown them her arm. Or if it was human it had to be a big kid at school: there was a lot had it in for Sally. And how did they know it wasn't a teacher? God, some of the teachers *she'd* had as a kid! Half killed you and nothing got said.

But Ms Partridge had an answer to everything. The shape of the bite. The size of the different tooth marks. How a doctor and a dentist could match it with the mouth that did it – and would, if need be. She ran the Lanes into dead ends, to places their stories couldn't go – till anger and frustration suddenly had Brian Lane bursting out with the truth.

'All right! I done it!' he shouted. 'Cleverpuss, ain't you? You don't know her, the little madam! She's trouble from the minute she wakes up to the minute she goes to bed!'

'Gave me a bad time from the off,' his wife said, patting her stomach as if Sally had committed some crime in the womb. 'Ought to be her middle name, Trouble. Never stopped crying, gave us a hell of a time, broken nights ...'

'She gets fed proper, gets dressed

nice … Then it's always after more –
want, want, want. Lies. Steals. We need a
lock on that fridge. Took the dog's dinner
once ….'

'A right little cat. There's no pleasing
her …'

Ms Partridge kept her eyes down and
took some notes, matter of fact.

But she wasn't the only one listening.
Sally was outside the door, hearing her
parents listing their love for her. And her
eyes glazed over, as if even the painful
bite couldn't hurt hard enough to keep
her sharp. As if nothing could hurt very
much against the Council being told all
this …

12

Kompel never knew quite what
happened. Some true stories aren't

wrapped up in endings for everyone taking part in them to read. She'd never actually known about the arm: not even all the teachers had known about that. And she didn't know about Social Services, nor how the school had only been waiting to jump onto something certain before calling them in.

But she did see something of the change she'd made by reading that false name from the hat, although she never knew it had anything to do with her.

All at once there were new dresses for everyone to see. And Sally walking with her sisters – and not being the one who did all the messages while the rest of them lay in bed.

And she was the May Queen, with her mother coming to clap her, all on her best behaviour. Sally Lane did that ever so well, Kompel thought – went through all the right moves and remembered where to stand. Almost smiled when a Championship footballer put the crown on her head; was very special for a day.

But Kompel never knew who helped to make sure it happened. Further up Clipper Street, though, some of the neighbours knew Ms Partridge and what her job was. They saw the regular car outside, noticed how the shouting from the Lanes' house got quieter, except when it was, 'Sally, *love*,' all very loud and clear.

And some of them knew about the deals Social Services did with people like the Lanes. *We'll help you, but only if you try.* We're keeping a good eye on you, and one step out of line, one more bruise or bump or bite or stripe and we'll throw the book at you – and see the mark *that* makes!

They knew Sally understood. How she

was on a deal, too. A deal to tell. There were to be no more dark secrets, not any more. She even had a number to ring.

And all at once, she had the power. She could get what she wanted some days with no more than a hard stare at the others. Things like biscuits, and sweets, and she even got to see what she wanted on the television. Well, the neighbours said, after what she's been through, didn't she deserve it?

But there wasn't any deal on love. Social Services couldn't quite make that happen.

13

Kompel worked on in the shop and she saw Sally Lane come in and go out, growing up, looking more and more people in the eye every day: even got given a hard look herself when she didn't get round to serving the girl fast enough. And once she heard Sally swearing at her father behind his Post Office grille. But she pretended not to see, not to hear. How could the girl know what was normal?

Kompel never regretted what she'd done that day in Assembly. And she would always be grateful to Mrs Peters for making it her secret, too. Because didn't you have to help Cinderellas like Sally? Make allowances for them?

And just hope that one day they might get the chance to start living happily ever after …

BOAT GIRL

1

The letter sent home had warned them that no-one went on the School Journey if a parent didn't come to the briefing. So there they were in the school hall, grown-up bottoms overlapping the rims of children's chairs, with just the one sitter who fitted her seat, and that was Kim Lung. She had to be there because her father's English wasn't up to such a meeting where all the details would be given out. He had to have a translator, even after all these years. Now he sat there holding Kim's hand and staring straight ahead, a short man with young hair, ready to dip his head to hers when the time came. Kim eased her hand away, pulled up her already pulled-up socks. She had come into the row of seats first, was on the wrong side of him; and she didn't like holding the hand with the scar on it. Her father let it drop, fingered the scar as he often did, like someone blind reading a story in it, while Kim looked up at all the adults' faces, feeling very out of place, very small.

The teachers came in and sat behind the table at the front. Mr Holt, the headteacher, nodded and smiled, especially at Kim. It was the look he gave the helpers and the parents, not the stare he usually gave the children.

Kim took in a long breath of hall air and sat up. No, feeling *small* wasn't it. She didn't feel small, she felt short, just miniature: because what she knew about some things was as much as anybody sitting there tonight.

'Letters,' Mr Holt said. It was near the end now and even Kim on her chair was uncomfortable. All the School Journey details had been given out and whispered in Vietnamese into her father's ear. It had to be done like this. She could speak the language well and understand it. Although she couldn't read it, it was all they spoke at home. She had to translate everything from school because her father couldn't read more than his name in English. There was never much put on paper at Kim's place.

'Letters.'

The important stuff was over. Kim made that little 'don't worry' sign translators do when they aren't going to bother. She could give the whispering a rest for a few minutes.

'Write often,' Mr Holt said. 'Children get very homesick if they don't get letters. Write any nonsense you want – but keep it cheerful.' Mr Holt made his old joke. 'Don't send sad stuff about going into their rooms and seeing the empty pillow. And if the cat dies tell them about the budgie instead!'

'What was that?' Kim's father demanded.

'Nothing much – about children feeling bad.'

Mr Lung looked at her. 'It isn't you feeling bad, it's me. No help for a week!'

And the meeting ended, with Kim only too glad that she didn't have to queue at the table to tell them about any medicines, or about wetting the bed. That was something! But not enough. Why couldn't her dad be the same as the rest?

2

She enjoyed the first night: six of them
in a little room in bunks, miles away in
Wales with a window where you could
see the river winding out of sight. A lot
better than the brick wall at the back of
the Odeon cinema that her bedroom faced
at home. And a load of laughs they had!
Tracy Sargent in a zip-up sleeping suit
which looked like an outsize babygro.
And Wendy Kent not having enough
hands to keep herself private when she
got undressed. It was better than sleeping
alone above the take-away. In loud
whispers they went on about Lee with
the ear-ring and a missing front tooth, the
boy they were all silly about. Until Mrs
Winterburn came in for the third time,
really ratty at the last in her dressing
gown and hairnet – and suddenly the air

became heavy, and loud breathing took over from talk. Kim was probably the last to sleep; she was more used to late nights than the rest, with the sounds from the take-away underneath her bedroom at home. She thought of her uncle at the counter and her father in the back, frying, sieving, banging the pans. And then the next thing she knew, it was day.

They went to the Big Pit, a disused Welsh coal-mine converted into a museum: which was not a line of smart underground show cases, but a real mine where the walls were dirty, the ceilings were low and the floor was uneven and trickled with water. Everyone wore a helmet with a modern Davy lamp, and it was very quiet under the hard hats as they went down in the big caged lift. Down, down, down, lower than going under the Thames tunnel, further down than anyone went up in the tower block lifts. And it was still very quiet as they walked along the 'roads' following their guide, who stooped as he would have had to stoop all the way to the pit face, going to dig coal. And when they were in a remote tunnel between two sets of closed fire doors he stopped, and said in his choky old Welsh voice, 'Now turn off your lamps, will you? See for yourselves a drop of total darkness ...'

The lights went off, each little searchlight on each hard head.

'You never see total darkness, you know. Not on the surface. There's always something, mind. But here you can't see a hand in front of your face. Can you?'

They tried – and they couldn't. The darkness was the blackest of blacks. It was awesome, had everybody silent for a bit, taking it in – a new experience,

something to make everyone think. It
was an instant in time when Kim's mind
went suddenly to when she'd heard
talk about total darkness before, when
she'd heard her father tell of it. Not
underground like now, not in the west,
but in a Vietnam night of a blackness
never known in Britain. She remembered
the talk about her mother and her father
hiding in the jungle, waiting with their
group of refugees for the men who
would lead them to the mother boat.
Twelve of them from the south who had
paid their gold to the old man in the
city, the twelve who had met up by the
sea and gone out in fishing boats to the
island off-shore. She remembered her
dad telling his brother of the moonless,
starless darkness which had been so
black, like now, that they had had to put
their hands on the shoulders in front,

so as not to get lost as they were led through the wet and slippery jungle. And how, to be counted by the boat man, they had had to stamp on the ground as they passed a certain spot because he couldn't see them.

And Kim had been there: not to be counted, but big in the total darkness of her mother's womb: knowing it only from what she had heard her father say afterwards.

As if suddenly attacked by a sharp pain, Kim shuddered, and in the dripping blackness of the mine she couldn't help but make the smallest of cries.

The lights came on.

'You all right, my pet? Wouldn't scare you for the world.'

'Scaredy-pants!'

But Kim didn't seem to hear what Wendy said. She was shaking off the old, dark thought. That wasn't what she'd come on the School Journey for, to feel bad.

3

By the time they got back to the grey stone house which was the School Journey Centre, it was time for the evening meal: all scraping chairs and passing the water and the clatter of cutlery on plates. It had been a long day and nobody was too faddy to leave any of the hot-pot, mash and baked beans. Whole loaves disappeared like slices and no-one cleared their mouths to even mention missing their television. In what had been the dining room of the country mansion, used to best silver and cut-glass, Dockside School ate fast: taking the next mouthful before finishing the last, eyes much sharper for seconds of food than for the letters being dished out.

The post had come: a thin pack in a thick rubber band which had been delivered while they were down the Big Pit. Not a lot of it, it was only their second day away, but some children's parents had thought ahead and got letters and cards off before the coach had left London.

'Just a few,' said Mr Brewer, giving them out. 'There'll be another post tomorrow ...'

Kim watched Wendy open hers: saw her not bothering with the letter so much as the fiver folded up in it. How could she? She watched Joss with his card written in black italic script, laughing at some joke. And she watched Lyndsey sniffing at her pink Snoopy paper with its triangle of kisses. Then it was Duty

Group, and washing up, and Kim was where she always spent a lot of her time – up to the wrists of her rubber gloves in a big kitchen sink, watching the suds.

4

The suds she watched the next day, though, were of a very different sort. Cold, frothing waves of them where they crashed in at the foot of the lifeboat cove. A glinty grey, the sea swelled itself up almost unseen, the wave shape becoming clear only at the last, just before it went thundering over the worn rocks.

The sea. Kim stared at it. She had never seen much of the sea. Her life had hardly taken her near it since she'd been born. She was much more used to the slow old Thames not far from the take-away – and that was very different from this. She stood apart and watched the water. She was held by it, because she knew it, the sea – in her bones, in her blood, in her soul. She was of the sea, was a true boat person: because Kim had been born on the mother boat.

She walked with the others round the lifeboat which had been designed to be so hard to sink. In its tight-fitting shed hung with medals and memorials to brave people, she looked at the sturdy craft, and she thought about that other one: the frail, overcrowded refugee boat. She thought about it in spite of herself, because she certainly didn't want to: no more than she'd wanted to think about that darkness in the Big Pit, which had started off all of this …

She remembered hearing her father telling his brother, when he had himself come to Britain. How he and her mother had been allowed on the mother boat with only the clothes they were wearing, everything else left behind on the island, every unnecessary weight, even the sandals from their feet. They had only been allowed the bottles of cough medicine everyone carried in their teeth, stuff to make them drowsy, to help them pass their difficult journey in sleep.

From high on the Welsh cliffs, Kim watched a small fishing boat bobbing out of the shelter of the cove. She heard the screams of the sea birds, each, it seemed, with its own individual voice. And inside her head she imagined again the shouts and the screams of the people in the mother boat being told to be quiet by the sailors. Adults packed into the bottom where it was roughest and sickest, the elderly in the middle and the youngest on the top. Parents and their children separated: and with so many clamouring to go, no mother being certain that her child had been allowed to follow on. Names being called, backwards and forwards: shrieks of grief when no answers came, and louder shouts of anger from the sailors. Her father had told his brother about it in a flat voice as though it were a fact of life. And he had thought himself lucky, he'd said, because Hoa had her baby inside her, and people pushed to give her a little more room.

'Ain't you ever seen the sea before?' Lee was next to her: but not acting as rough as his voice. He was staring at the waves, too; and he put a hand on her shoulder.

'Not much,' Kim said. And she was pleased he hadn't said it gentle, or she might have wanted to cry: not the point of a School Journey at all.

5

They were late back from the coast that evening and the warden wasn't pleased about it at all. Mrs Winterburn never grovelled to anyone, but she did go red when she saw the woman waiting for them at the front door. She shouted at the children to hurry – and she ended up serving the potatoes herself. So there was no time for the games on the field and in the woods that they'd been promised. It was wash up, diaries and bed.

And letters. They had time to get the post given out. Mr Brewer brought it round proudly as if he'd written it all himself – a fatter batch tonight with two rubber bands, one going each way.

The people who had had one the night before all had another, and most of the rest had one, too. There were posh-looking letters and scruffy-looking letters; there were long ones and short ones; there were some with drawings put in by little brothers and sisters, some with money. Some were in capital letters all through and didn't keep to the lines, some were faint and scrawly, and one was done on a computer. They came on white paper, on blue paper, on pink and rainbow: they were torn out, ripped off and crinkly-edged.

And nearly everyone got one. But Lee didn't, and neither did Kim. 'Early days,' said Mr Brewer. 'Tomorrow, eh?'

Kim went to bed, tucked in early, and turned her back on all the rude talk going on. The others thought she was too stuck up, but it wasn't that. She just couldn't forget that sea. She couldn't get out of her mind how that fishing boat in the Welsh cove had gone up and down on the water like a wooden fork in her washing-up. She couldn't get out of her head the imaginary picture she had of her mother; imaginary because they hadn't even brought sandals, let alone a photograph. And she began to get cross at her dad. Here she was, filled with sad thoughts which made her miss him – and he hadn't sent her a letter. All the children except two had heard from their homes, and she had to be one of the two! All of their parents were busy people, it wasn't just him. You could see how a lot of them had had a struggle with their ball-points and the paper. So why couldn't he have tried? It didn't need much. What sort of a father was he?

6

It was good in the back seat of the coach, going to the farm. Especially for Kim because she wasn't really a back-seat person, she was much more of an up-front passenger. She didn't fight for a very front seat or to sit next to a teacher, but she did like to be where she could hear what they said, and look at the things they pointed out. She'd sit next to anyone – she often had to, because she wasn't one of those glued to the same partner, but she was surprised when it was Lee who shouted, 'Come on, Kim – up the back with me!'

And she'd gone. That had surprised her a bit, too. Wendy went, and Tracy Sargent, and Jimmy and a couple of others. But it was Lee who made the fun, the one they really wanted to be

with, and it was Kim who he'd pushed
in beside him, squashed her beside the
window.

Wendy didn't like it, that was as clear
as a sheet of cling-film. She mucked about
all right, so did Tracy, and they had a lot
of laughs with Lee. But she didn't like
it because most of what Lee said went
Kim's way. And although she gave him
plenty of room for sliding closer, it was
Kim he kept tight-to in the corner.

It was the letters, Kim decided: that
was why he was being friendly. She
hadn't had one, and he hadn't had one.
But whatever the reason, Wendy Kent
and Tracy Sargent didn't like it: they
didn't like it one bit, staring at each other
every time Kim spoke as if they didn't
understand a word she said.

They liked the farm more. They forgot
the coach for a bit when they went all

soft over some of the animals, and it was very hard not to, with the newborn lambs like babies' toys, and the day-old calves like Bambis. They all went potty over one lamb which was being reared by another lamb's mother.

'That one's mother died,' the girl from the farm told them. 'But she's been accepted by that ewe.'

'Aah! I'll have her,' said Mr Brewer. 'Trust *ewe!* Get it? Ewe!'

They laughed. Mrs Winterburn was human after all: she'd cracked a joke! Everyone laughed except Kim – because in spite of herself she was having another of those sudden quiet moments; it was as if she was walking into them. She really didn't dwell on things as a rule – she got on. She worked hard at school and she worked hard at home, downstairs in the take-away. Bed-time for her was never for staring at the ceiling and thinking about things, it was head on the pillow, turn over and sleep – usually in seconds. This week was turning out differently, though: this week, standing and staring were part of the programme. And for her it was standing and staring and remembering ...

Her mother had died, on the mother boat. Like the little lamb, Kim had been left to someone else to get her over those first dangerous days. She'd heard all about that through a thin wall, too. How, pregnant, hungry and worn out by the struggle and the strain of the escape, her mother had started having her on the boat, weeks early. How the boat had hit heavy seas and people had been thrown about and crushed in the tossing and rolling. How Kim had been born and her mother had died. And how another woman with a young child had shared her breast milk.

'Baa! You look like one of them. Don't she look like one of them, staring?' Wendy Kent was a bad enemy to make.'Sheep-face!'

Big Eddie, the one Wendy was talking to, smirked his smirk. 'Baa!' he agreed.

'Cleverest thing you've said all week,' Kim told him. And her back stayed straight: because she was her mother's daughter, and this sort of thing was nothing to what that brave woman had gone through.

7

There was time for games that night, up on the sloping meadow they called the sports field. Organised games: football and rounders, until three rounders balls had been lost in the undergrowth on the edge and they started asking for something else. Hide-and-seek in the thick woods above them.

'Tomorrow, the last night,' promised Mr Brewer. 'Can't be late for supper twice.'

They were kept waiting to go in for their meal: a bit of pay-back from the warden, probably. But while they queued, to stop them getting noisier and noisier, Mr Brewer came down the line with the letters which had come that day. And it was a very thick handful. Eyes really stared, everyone's eyes, even those of people pretending to look the other way. And there seemed to be something for everyone. For some it was the third and fourth they'd had – and it was the first for a red-faced Lee, whose tooth-gap smile would have made a photograph worth framing.

Something for everyone, it seemed, except Kim. At the meal table with only her plate to concentrate on, she found it hard to get her food down. All the talk around her was of London and what was going on at home; pets and grans and the telly; everyone showing this bit and that in their letters: all whispered secrets and loud jokes and ketchup on the envelopes. Debbie had got a letter from a boy she said she didn't like in Year Five, written somewhere private on lavatory paper. Pulling it out too quickly, she had to share it with her table, every soppy page ending 'NOW PLEASE WASH YOUR HANDS'. Mrs Winterburn read out her husband's views on the new council swimming pool: and Mr Brewer tucked a letter down his jumper. But there was nothing for Kim, not until the teachers noticed and they found a postcard from Mr Holt for her to be in charge of.

It gave her indigestion, her disappointment. Her rotten dad! How old was she? How long had he been in England? Couldn't he have put himself out to learn enough English in ten years to write 'Dear Kim. Love from Dad' – how hard was that to do? It was all she wanted. He could have sent his signature written sideways down one of their menus and made her feel good. But nothing: he'd sent nothing. He was a great failure. Why couldn't he try harder and find the guts to go to English classes, even if they were difficult? Why did he always have to lean on her? What sort of a rotten father was he?

'Oi! Kim – what's this say?'

It was Lee. They'd been dismissed and he had found her in the little ornamental garden with the view of the sparkling valley: the quiet place with no ball games allowed where no-one went. He had got his mother's letter, was still grinning with it – but he couldn't read it very well.

Kim helped him. And, somehow, it helped her. In spite of her dark mood, she found herself settling into it. It was interesting how people were different. She had a dad and no mum; Lee had a mum and no dad. The letter was all about the music charts and what was happening in the serials. A different life from hers. And the letter ended with more kisses than Kim could count.

There was a secret sound from the rockery above them.

'Here they are! Look at them two! Know you now!'

Kim needn't have looked to know whose jealous voice that was: Wendy –

pointing, sneering, twisting up her face. Why? She was only helping Lee, it wasn't any more than that. But before she could explain it, try to make friends again, Wendy went. She pulled Tracy away as if she had something urgent to do. Probably something nasty to Kim's bed.

'Cheers, mate.' And Lee had gone, too.

The sun was casting shadows on the valley now, the sparkle had gone from this place. Kim went to the kitchen to help Mr Brewer with the cocoa. And then she went to check her bed. But all Wendy ended up doing was to ignore it, with Kim in it. She talked loudly all round her, and was careful not to answer the couple of quiet words Kim said.

8

The next day they went to the castle at

Goodrich. But they'd been round a lot of places by then – and what really had them buzzing was the 'wide game' when they got back. Not just ordinary hide-and-seek, Mr Brewer promised, but something bigger, with teams and proper rules. It was to be their last night there: no diaries and follow-up work as everyone went up to the field.

Mr Brewer explained it all carefully. Half the group were to go off into the woods to hide. They'd be quite safe, he told them: the woods were bounded by a strong fence on their further side so there was no danger of anyone wandering off the site. The other half would count a hundred and then go out looking for them, with a few good tacklers staying behind to guard the home base – which was Mrs Winterburn and the anoraks. Every hider who got back scored a point.

Everyone who was 'had' gave a point to the hunting side. And anyone who stayed hidden till the end scored half a point when the three whistles sounded.

Those were the rules, and Kim was herded by Mr Brewer's arm into one of the groups of prey. She didn't play out of doors much where she lived, her father wouldn't let her, so this was something different. When the whistle went for the start, she ran off fast with the others, high-stepped in her wellingtons through the stingers and the fern, and quickly decided on a course of her own to the left. Everyone who went together would get found together, she reckoned. She could get a point on her own. With a quick look back over her shoulder to check who was watching who, who was going where, she disappeared into the darkness of the woods. But already her heart had sunk – because what she had seen when she looked round was Wendy and Tracy and Big Eddie coming out to the edge of the group that was left, on her side of the field. So! Her new enemies were going to be her hunters.

They weren't pointing, they weren't showing which way they were looking, but Kim knew very well who those three were going to come after: it was definitely going to be her. She was their target, she was going to be their prey. And who would care about the rules? The real idea, what they'd really be after, was to find her, and get her and hurt her – accidentally push her over in the nettles, something like that. She knew from the way they'd been standing smiling – all casual and pretending not to look – that hurting her was what their game was all about.

She ran hard through the moist and slippery wood, quickly decided to go off the wide path onto the narrow track. Then off the narrow track into the undergrowth till she was crashing through tangles of bush and spiders' webs. The voices of the other hiders went distant as she looked desperately for a place well away from where Wendy might look. All she could hear as she jumped and pushed was the thump of her heart and the sounds of the fears in her head. She didn't want a quick run-in. The last thing she was after now was a point. All she wanted was to stay hidden and to get safely back to supper without any kicking or punching or scratching or stinging: without any of the things those others were out to do to her.

Cleverly, it struck her as she ran that her best protection might be the very thing she was frightened of: nettles and thorns. If she didn't like them, the hunters wouldn't either, would they? Getting tired now, legs heavy in her boots, she saw what she thought might do. Coming at it by a roundabout way so as not to show where she'd gone, Kim crept and crawled and weaved herself into the biggest blackberry bush she could find. A blackberry bush very dense and prickly, a careful hiding place where she daren't move once she was lying there because to move would be to scratch herself badly. She lay there, thought of a million better places the way hiders do, but knew she had to stick with that one. And like that, trembling, Kim waited.

'We're right here! We know you're there! Give up! Come on, give up!'

'Can you hear us? It's you we're coming for!'

Was it bluff? Mental warfare? Which way were the footsteps coming?

9

They came her way. Wendy Kent and Tracy Sargent came with a grudge against her over Lee, bringing Big Eddie with them to do what they wanted. And from their voices when she heard them in the distance, she knew she'd been right over what they were about.

'Snobby little dilk!'

'Show-off! Anyhow, all sorts happen when you fall over!'

'Yeah, bad luck, eh?!'

They laughed, looking forward to hurting her.

'Only be her word against ours!'

And then it was Wendy in a witch voice with the worst of hide-and-seek scares, calling out. 'We know you're here! You can hear us, can't you? We're coming to get you!'

Kim didn't move. She couldn't be sure how well she'd tucked her left foot under the bush behind her, but she knew she couldn't shift it. She couldn't make a movement, not run the risk of a sound. They were getting closer now, only metres away; they'd done horribly well to follow her trail. She could hear their breathing, could almost feel their strong will to find her and hurt her. In despair she clawed her fingers into the cold soil, allowed an insect into her ear, stopped breathing normally and took shallow breaths which wouldn't move her back. It wasn't what she wanted to do.

She wanted to jump up and scream. Instead, it was a fight to stay still. But she fought hard, made her eyes know the

sight, her nostrils the smell, her mouth
the taste of the earth she was pressed so
hard against.

And lying there, not thinking about
anything but her fear, she knew for sure
what it had been like on that island
in Vietnam. Not from the stories she'd
heard when her father told his brother,
but from being pressed against the earth
right here. She could have been her
father, and these hunters could have been
the North Vietnamese soldiers brought
south to stop him getting away from that
island, searching the jungle with orders to
capture or to kill.

She could have been her father lying
there, his wife beside him, both scared to
death in the pitch darkness. The soldiers
wouldn't be blamed for killing, these
guards crashing through the foliage with
their weapons ready to use.

'You hear us, Kim Lung? We're gonna get you!'

Closer. Very close. A sudden risked move, the lift of an eye. And the sight of the toe-cap of a boot so close the stitching could be counted. A cringe, a wait for the shout, for the blow – but holding the breath, fighting not to panic.

But it would only be a fist, or a boot. It wouldn't be a bayonet. It wouldn't be what her father had had: a bayonet stabbing down into the dense foliage and into his hand, into the flesh between his finger and his thumb; pinning him to the rotting earth while still he didn't shout; holding it, twisting it, then pulling it away to be stabbed into the next big plant – only the darkness hiding the blood on the soldier's bayonet.

Kim's heart beat enough to lift her body from the ground. She closed her eyes again, did her screaming inside her head, like her father had done.

And then suddenly it wasn't a scream but a whistle which sounded, three blessed times. And crashing away on a run-in from some distant place of his own came Lee, whooping in a winning way.

'Didn't get me! Half a point, I got!'

'Stupid game!' said Big Eddie. 'Get a football out, eh?'

'Yeah.'

The two boys went off: so did Wendy and Tracy, after one last hard look round.

'Thought she'd come this way.'

'Done a double back.'

'Yeah. Leave it.'

They ran off. But it was a very long time before Kim could emerge. It seemed to take her a lifetime to come crawling out of that hiding place.

10

When the coach drew up at the school everyone on the pavement waved as if it were a royal visit. Dogs had come, and push-chairs with little brothers and sisters. Mr Holt, the headteacher, was there, smiling a welcome. But it was the parents' faces everyone wanted to see. No eyes were ever sharper than in that first look along Dockside Street for the people they lived with.

Kim, too: eyes sharper today than anyone's. And he was there, her father, smiling shyly, waving his hand in a small and private way. Kim saw him and didn't push to be first off the coach. She didn't need to. He was there, everything was all right, she could wait. She looked out of the window as she queued in the aisle, and she waved again. Back came another smile, an ordinary smile, a smile with nothing of an apology for not writing, just pleased to see her.

She blew him a little kiss. Well, it was her fault, too, wasn't it? She'd worked it out last night. She hadn't bothered to translate that bit about the letters, what the head had said at the end of the meeting. She'd had enough by then – so how was he to know? And she hadn't thought she'd *need* a letter from him. She could easily have left him with a couple of envelopes already addressed: but she hadn't thought she'd miss him.

At last her turn came. She jumped off the coach and surprised him with her hug, almost pulled him over. He hugged her in return and took a step back, shook his head at her. Well, why should he understand this loving? He wasn't to know this was her secret way of saying sorry for those bad thoughts she'd had about him. He wasn't to know what she knew now – that he wasn't a man of words and writing, but a man of action. A brave man those years ago, and a strong man now. No-one remembered what had happened in Vietnam any more: no-one seemed to know, even, or to care. But Kim did. She understood it now. And as they walked to the bus, she made sure he had her case in his good hand, and she changed places on the pavement, to get a tight hold on his bayonet scar.

'Like a number of long established authors of a broad range of much admired books, Bernard Ashley has found that some books which are standard as a focus for his school-visits have slipped to out-of-print unavailability. So Ashley Chappel are bringing some of his own books out in new editions and one of these is *Your Guess is as Good as Mine*. In the primary school where I was headteacher I had this extremely useful book in a parents' library as well as copies shelved for youngsters own reading. The theme is stranger-danger and the treatment is in effect a long short-story. The text now appears slightly updated and the story retains the elements of being direct, dramatic, relevant, totally plausible and highly effective …Also from the same source and for ages 6ish upwards is *Justin and the Demon Drop Kick* with a head's moment of footie fun leading to entertaining repercussions.'

Chris Brown, School Librarian

Coming soon. Look out for -

JACK AND THE GERMAN SPY

It's 1939 and the war's beginning. Everyone's afraid of spies.

When Jack tumbles off the Kent train with the other wartime evacuees from London, no one in the village wants to take him in. Then Lady Ashwell patriotically sweeps him off to the Hall, where Jack learns how to hold a knife and fork and her son Clive learns how to fight dirty – and when events in the night turn nasty, the boys team up to unmask a sinister enemy.